LITTLE LEFTY

LITTLE
LEFTY

MATT CHRISTOPHER

BellaRosaBooks

LITTLE LEFTY
ISBN 978-1-933523-38-5
2009 Reprint Edition by Bella Rosa Books

LCCN: 2009942414

Previously Published in the U.S.A. by Little, Brown & Company. First hardback: 1959. Paperback: 1993; ISBN 0-316-14100-3.

Printed in the United States of America on acid-free paper.

Cover illustration by Jack Ross.

BellaRosaBooks and logo are trademarks of Bella Rosa Books

10   9   8   7   6   5   4   3   2   1

1

The late June sun was hot on Bill Bailey's face. Every once in a while he whirled the tattered baseball glove around on his hand.

"Come on, Sack! Come on!" yelled Bucky Myers, the right-hander who sat beside Bill. "Ram that ball down their throats!"

Bill and Bucky were the same age, but Bill was so small that he looked two or three years younger. He had known, since baseball season had started, that he'd be lucky to even get on the Blackhawks' roster. His only chance was that he was left-handed, and he could throw a ball harder than a lot of kids his age.

1

Sack, the batter, swung at a high pitch.

"Bring 'em down, Sack!" Bucky yelled. "Make 'em come to you!" He looked at Bill and the other players on the bench. "Wake up you guys! Let's hear some noise!"

Bill wet his lips. "Get a hit, Sack! Get on! Come on, babe!"

His voice was drowned out by the others, and he stopped yelling. He didn't feel like yelling anyway. He didn't even feel like sitting here and watching the game. What fun was there watching a game when what he wanted most was to play?

Another pitch and Sack whiffed. He carried the bat to the bench with him, handed it to Jamie, the mascot, and sat down without looking at anybody.

Eddie Christiansen, the right fielder, poked a hot grounder to short. The short-stop fumbled the ball and Eddie made first on an error.

Bill looked at the scoreboard at the right side of the field. The Blackhawks had scored three runs in the first inning. The three goose eggs after that began to look bigger and bigger compared to the Eagles' six runs. The Eagles had scored two runs in the first, none in the second, and four in the third.

Catcher Tommy Wiggins was up next for the Blackhawks. He walloped a fly to second. The second baseman zipped the white pill to first, throwing out Eddie before he could tag up.

Three outs.

Now, thought Bill. Maybe now Manager Hanley will let me pitch.

But Manager Frank Hanley didn't say anything to him. Bucky Myers went out to the mound and struck out the first batter. The next hitter fouled two pitches against the backstop screen, then lined one out to left for two bases.

Bill knew he could do better than

Bucky. Those Eagles' players were knocking Bucky all over the lot.

The next Eagles' batter bunted. Bucky fielded the ball. Threw to first for a fast out.

"Two outs, Bucky, boy!" the team shouted. "Let's get the next one!"

But Bucky threw three wild pitches before he put one over. The fifth pitch gave the batter a free ticket to first.

Crack! A fast bounding ball to Donny Swanson at third. He snagged the ball in his glove, stepped on the bag, and the rough inning was over.

The fifth inning went by scoreless for both teams. The Eagles still led, 6 to 3.

The Blackhawks had one more chance to win. The boys were quiet as they sat on the bench and watched their hitter put on his helmet and walk to the plate. The saddest of them all was Bill. He was the only one of the fifteen players on the roster who hadn't played in the game yet.

He sat back with his arms crossed over his chest, his black and yellow cap tilted back on his dark-haired head.

The hitter was second baseman Corky Davis. He slashed at a high pitch. The ball zoomed straight up into the air, curved behind the plate as it came down. The Eagles' catcher knocked of his mask, staggered under the ball, and made the catch.

"Bill!" said Manager Hanley. "Bill Bailey! Pinch-hit for Donny!"

Bill stared. Manager Hanley was poking a finger at him. "Yes, you, Bill. Pick up a club and stand at the plate till he gets a strike on you."

Bill laid aside his glove. He rose from the bench, found his favorite bat. He pushed his cap into his pants pocket, put on the protective helmet, and stepped to the plate.

"Ball one!"

Then, "Strike!"

5

The third pitch was in there. Bill cut hard. The ball arched out to deep second. The Eagles' second baseman trotted back, raised his glove hand, and snared the ball for the out. Bill was halfway down the first-base line when he saw the catch. He stopped running and turned disgustedly back toward the bench.

Kenny Ayers popped to the pitcher, and the game was over. The Eagles had won, 6 to 3.

Bill walked away from the ball park alone. Maybe the team didn't want him because he was so small. But being small wasn't his fault, was it? Anyway, even though he was small. His arm was just as strong as anybody else's on the team.

"Hey, Bill, wait a minute!"

The high, thin voice startled Bill. He turned and saw Larry Fowler run up beside him. Larry was a lot taller than

Bill. He didn't like baseball.

He straightened his dark-rimmed glasses on his nose and looked at Bill with wide, steady eyes.

"You only got into the game a minute, didn't you?" he said. "Just to pinch-hit."

Bill looked away. "That's right," he said softly.

"You know what I'd do? I'd quit, that's what I'd do."

Bill tightened his lips. "You would?"

"Yes, I would. What good is it to sit on the bench all game and just bat once? I wouldn't go for it. Not me."

Bill thought a moment.

"That's what I was thinking, too. Larry," he said finally. "That's exactly what I was thinking."

2

"Let's go swimming, Bill. That's more fun."

Bill smacked his fist hard into the oiled pocket of his glove. "Okay. After I take off this jersey."

Larry's eyes widened. "You're going to give the jersey back to Frank Hanley, aren't you?"

"I suppose I'll have to," said Bill, "If I'm not going to play any more."

"Sure, you'll have to," replied Larry. "I don't think he would want you to pitch, anyway, Bill. You're too small."

"I know," said Bill.

He went home. His mother asked him who had won the game. He told her that the Eagles had.

"Did you pitch at all?" she asked. She was a tall, pretty woman with blond hair. She was in the kitchen, ironing clothes. Mrs. Swanson, whose son played third for the Blackhawks, was sitting at the table, a cup of coffee in front of her. Almost every night one or two of the ladies would come over and spend an hour or so with Bill's mother. Bill's father had died in an automobile accident a long time ago, so she had to work during the day to support herself and Bill.

"No, I didn't pitch," Bill said. "I only pinch-hit, and I got out."

Mrs. Swanson smiled. "Well, you'll have your chance again, Bill. How did Donny do?"

"He got a hit," Bill said. "I guess that's all."

He went to his room, took off his yellow

and black jersey with Blackhawks print-ed across the front of it, and got his bathing trunks. He and Larry picked up Larry's trunks and walked to the pool.

A dozen boys and girls were in the water. Some were playing with a large rubber ball. A lifeguard was sitting on top of a high platform.

A man was sitting on a bench near the bathhouse. He was smoking a pipe and watching the kids. Bill remembered that he had seen the man at the ball game.

Bill and Larry entered the bathhouse and changed into their trunks. They hung their clothes in lockers. Larry laid his glasses on the top shelf. Then they went outside. Larry was the first to leap off the diving board.

Bill held his nose and jumped. Splash! Water sprayed in all directions as he landed. It felt cold against his skin. He almost went to the bottom.

He rose to the surface, whipped his

wet hair away from his face, and breathed in a lungful of fresh air.

"Hey, Bill!" Larry yelled. "Let's play follow-the-leader!"

"Okay!"

Larry swam with an overhand stroke to the opposite side of the pool. Bill followed him. Larry ducked his head underwater. His feet raised up out of the water, then followed the rest of him out of sight. Bill took a deep breath and pushed himself underwater, too. The water was clear as a crystal. Bill could see Larry swimming ahead of him.

Then Larry swam to the surface. Bill came up, too.

Suddenly a pain shot through Bill's right leg. His head went under for a moment. He pushed himself up again, spat water out of his mouth.

"Larry!" he screamed. "Larry!"

3

Larry turned. He was almost at the other side of the pool. His eyes widened as he looked at Bill.

"Larry!" Bill screamed again. "My— my leg! Help!"

Bill tried to rub his leg with his hand. His head went under. His mouth filled with water again. He pushed himself up and spat it out.

Larry swam hard toward him. He cut through the water like a fish.

Just then Bill heard a splash. He shot a quick glance at the platform where the lifeguard had sat. It was empty. Then Bill saw the lifeguard taking long, powerful strokes through the water toward him.

Larry reached Bill first. "Get on my back!" he yelled.

Bill obeyed. Boy, that leg hurt.

Larry swam a little ways with Bill, then began to puff hard.

The lifeguard reached them. "Let me take him," he said to Larry.

Larry didn't object. The lifeguard held Bill upon the water with one arm, and stroked with the other. In a little while they reached the ladder at the edge of the pool. The lifeguard climbed up, carrying Bill. Water dripped off their bodies.

He laid Bill down on the soft grass. "What happened?" he asked.

"I guess I caught a cramp in my right leg," murmured Bill weakly.

Bill saw that the man on the bench had come over and was watching. He wasn't smoking now. The bowl of his pipe was sticking out over the edge of his shirt pocket.

The lifeguard rubbed Bill's leg gently.

Slowly the pain began to disappear.

After a while the lifeguard smiled at Bill. "How does it feel now?"

"Much better." Bill smiled back. He looked at Larry. A happy, relieved grin was on Larry's face.

"I guess I would've drowned if it weren't for you and Larry," said Bill to the lifeguard.

The lifeguard grinned. "That's all right. That's what I'm here for." He turned to Larry. "Here's the fellow who deserves a lot of credit, though. He held you up long enough for me to get to you. I didn't hear or see you right away with this crowd and noise we have today." He stopped rubbing Bill's leg. "Feel okay now?"

Bill nodded. "Yes. Thanks a lot."

The lifeguard helped him to his feet, then walked away and climbed to his seat atop the platform.

● ● ●

The man with the pipe in his pocket still stood there. He was big and husky. His hair was brown with streaks of gray at the sides. The man grinned at Bill.

"Hi, Bill," he said. "That was a close call."

Bill smiled. "It sure was."

"My name is Ray Colby," said the man. "I saw you pitch the other day. You looked pretty good."

"He's not playing any more," Larry cut in.

The man's smile vanished. "Why not?"

"He's too small. They won't give him a chance."

Ray Colby looked at Bill. A frown knitted his brow. "I don't think Bill should quit because he's too small. A lot of ballplayers—"

"He doesn't like baseball anyway," Larry interrupted. He looked darkly at Ray Colby, then took Bill's arm. "Come on, Bill. Let's get changed."

A puzzled look came over Ray Colby's face. He turned to Larry, but Larry was already heading for the bath-house.

They went into the building and changed into their clothes. Bill was fin-ished dressing before Larry and started putting on his shoes. Larry seemed to be dressing slowly on purpose.

At last Larry was ready. They walked outside together. Ray Colby was back on the bench, smoking his pipe.

He's nice, thought Bill. He saw me pitch the other day. He remembered me.

Bill and Larry walked along silently for a while. Goose pimples formed on Bill's arm as the horrible thought of having nearly drowned filled his mind. Bill would never have believed that Larry would have done anything like saving somebody's life. The greatest thing a guy could do.

I'll owe him something for that, thought Bill. I'll owe something as long as I live.

Larry looked at him. His face broke into a warm smile. "How would you like to have a ship-in-a-bottle?" Larry said brightly. "A Spanish galleon?"

Bill's eyebrows arched. "You—you mean you have one that you'll give me?"

"Of course!"

"Golly! I don't know."

"I'll give it to you," said Larry. "It's a beauty."

They went to Larry's house. The ship-in-a-bottle was on a shelf in Larry's bedroom. It was indeed a beauty. The wide part of the bottle was about eight inches long, the neck about three.

"Boy!" Bill gasped. "How did you get the ship in there, Larry?"

A proud grin spread over Larry's face.

"You have to use thread," he said. "It's tough, but it's a lot of fun."

Larry took the bottle off the shelf. "Here, Bill. It's yours."

Bill was excited. "You're sure you want to give it to me, Larry? You're really sure?"

"I'm really sure," said Larry. "You're my best friend. That's why I'm giving it to you, Bill."

Bill took the bottle. He looked at the model ship inside it, a Spanish galleon that looked so real you would think that wee little men were inside of it. Bill had never been given anything so wonderful in all his life.

"Thanks, Larry." He swallowed. "Maybe Mom will put a shelf in my room like yours. I'll put the ship on it. I'll never forget the gift. And I'll never forget that you saved my life, Larry. Never."

"That's all right, Bill." Larry's eyes

shone. "You—you won't play baseball any more, will you, Bill? You'll just play with me."

Bill looked long at Larry. That was sure asking a lot. But Larry had saved his life, and Larry wanted him for his friend.

"Okay, Larry," said Bill. "I promise I'll never play baseball any more."

4

Tommy Wiggins stopped at Bill's house early the next afternoon. Tommy was tall and husky. He was wearing his Blackhawks jersey and baseball cap.

"Hi Bill, he greeted, holding his catcher's mitt with a ball in it. "Get your glove. We're going down to the field to practice."

Bill stared at him. He was surprised to think that any of the players would stop in to see him about baseball practice. He hardly played enough for anybody to know that he was a member of the team.

"I don't think I want to go, Tommy," Bill answered after he thought awhile.

Tommy frowned. "Why not? You

play a little in every game. Come on. Get your glove."

The desire to go with Tommy grew inside Bill. Yet, at the same time, Bill remembered that he had made a promise to Larry Fowler. He had promised Larry he would not play baseball again.

He didn't know what to do.

"Make up your mind," said Tommy impatiently. "Are you coming, or aren't you? You'll never make a ballplayer if you don't practice, you know."

Bill wet his lips. What a spot to be in! Deep inside he loved baseball. He enjoyed standing on the pitcher's mound. He enjoyed winding up and throwing the ball as hard as he could at the plate. It was fun trying to fool the batter by throwing a hook. Of course, the hook didn't always work. And quite often it did not go over the plate. But sometimes the hitter would swing at the ball and miss. That was the fun in pitching.

It was fun standing in the batter's box, too. Bill loved the feel of the shiny, smooth bat. He enjoyed cutting at the ball, the solid crack that resounded throughout the park when bat met ball, the run to first base.

He loved every bit of baseball.

Bill's heart knocked against his ribs.

"Just a minute, Tommy," he said breathlessly. "I'll put on my jersey and get my glove."

They walked to the ballfield together. Most of the Blackhawks were already there. Mr. Hanley knocking out fly balls to the outfielders. The rest of the team were playing pitch and catch.

Ray Colby was sitting on the bottom step of the grandstand behind the back-stop screen. He was smoking a pipe. Bill and Tommy had to walk in front of the screen to get to the first-base side of the field, where the team's equipment was.

"Hello, Bill," Ray said as the boys walked by. "How are you today?"

Bill smiled. "Hello, Mr. Colby. I'm fine, thanks."

Mr. Colby must sure love baseball, thought Bill. He seemed to be at the ball park most of the time.

Tommy picked a brand-new baseball out of the canvas bag. "I'll warm you up, Bill." Maybe Mr. Hanley will have you throw 'em in for batting practice."

They worked out together for five minutes or so. Then Mr. Hanley called for all the baseballs to be brought in.

"We'll have batting practice," he said. His eyes settled on Bill, then on Bucky Myers. He tossed two balls to Bucky. "Throw 'em in for a while, Bucky. Then I'll have Bill throw. Shag some flies till your turn comes, Bill."

Bill ran happily out to the outfield. He misjudged a ball, but caught two high ones. Then he batted. He laid down a bunt and knocked hot grounders to the infielders.

When Bill started pitching for batting practice he had trouble getting the ball over the plate.

"Hit the target!" yelled Tommy, who was catching. He held his mitt up big and round. "Hit the target!"

Bill stretched, delivered. He aimed for Tommy's mitt. The ball sped straight for the heart of the plate. Then *crack!* A line drive to left field.

The next pitch was directed almost in the same place. The batter swung hard and missed.

"That's the way to throw the ball in there!" Tommy cried.

Suddenly a tall dark figure with glasses approached around the side of the grandstand. Bill went limp as he saw his friend, Larry Fowler, look directly at him. Larry's eyes were like black stones, his mouth a straight, hard line.

Bill threw a wild pitch. Again he threw wild, almost hitting the batter. Then he lobbed one in. The ball struck the plate. Tommy caught it on the hop.

"Okay, Bill," said Frank Hanley. "That's enough. You're getting tired." He called in first baseman Dave Sawyer to continue throwing.

Bill was glad to stop. He felt that he should not have practiced at all. He had gone against his word to Larry.

5

Bill's heart was heavy. He walked over to Larry. Larry's mouth was closed tightly. His lips quivered a little.

"Tommy asked me to come," said Bill.

Larry's lips parted. "You promised," he said.

"I know. I'm sorry, Larry. But Tommy kept talking, and I felt I just had to come. That's all."

Ray Colby rose from the other end of the stands and came toward them. Larry saw him and touched Bill's arm.

"Let's go," he said, and started to walk away.

"Bill!" Ray Colby called. "Wait a

minute!"

Bill paused. He couldn't walk away from Ray Colby. Why did Larry want him to do that?

Larry sure acted funny every time Mr. Colby was around.

"Why are you leaving?" Ray Colby asked. "You're not that tired, are you?"

Bill shook his head. "No."

Larry was still walking toward the rear of the grand stand. Every once in a while he looked back.

"Your last name is Bailey, isn't it?" Ray Colby smiled.

Bill nodded. He wondered how Mr. Colby knew his name, and why Mr. Colby seemed so interested in him. "That's right. Bill Bailey," he said.

"And you think you can't be a pitcher because you're so small," Mr. Colby went on.

Bill shrugged. "Maybe when I get older and bigger I could be."

"Yes. But you're old enough to start now. Years ago, when I could still play ball, I used to catch for one of the best pitchers in our league. He was small too, and he was a southpaw, just like you. We called him Little Lefty. But he was a big man when it came to pitching. Husky six-footers would come to the plate and go down swinging just like anybody else. He had the stuff. And you know what gave him the stuff? Pluck. Determination. That's the only way you can get what you want, Bill. You have to work for it. And the time to start is when you're a kid. Come with me. I have a glove and ball in my car. We'll play some pitch and catch."

Larry turned around. His brows knitted sharply as he looked at Bill. "You coming with me, Bill, or are you staying here?"

"Wait a few minutes, Larry. We won't play much. Will we, Mr. Colby?"

Ray Colby looked thoughtfully at Larry, then smiled at Bill. "No. I just want to show you a couple of things about pitching. Straighten you out on a few things when you're in the box."

He got his glove and ball from the car, then scratched a mark into the soft dirt with the toe of his shoe.

"Did you ever pitch, Mr. Colby?" Bill asked.

"Call me Ray." Mr. Colby smiled. "No. I never pitched. But being a catcher I learned a lot about pitching. Especially from Little Lefty. Now," he said, drawing Bill's attention to the mark he had made, "let's say this is the rubber. Nobody is on. You're left handed, so you put your left foot on the rubber, and your right foot behind it. Hold the ball in your left hand, and get the signal from your catcher. When you have the signal, stretch, turn"—Ray Colby went through the motions as he explained how to do it—"swing your right foot in front of the rubber, and pivot your left foot. Then throw. . . . Let me go through that again."

Ray Colby went through the motions again, and repeated everything almost word for word.

"All right. Try it yourself," he said.

Bill took the ball from Ray and did everything exactly the way Ray did. Bill was very happy, because it was the first time anybody had ever shown him how to stand correctly in the pitcher's box.

"I'm going home!" cried Larry suddenly.

Bill looked at him. Larry was hurt. Bill squeezed the ball hard in his hand.

Larry had done more for him than a lot of fellows would do for their friends. Saving Bill's life was a great thing in itself. But besides that Larry had given Bill one of his most prized possessions, a ship-in-a-bottle. A ship Larry had made himself . . . He had probably spent hours and hours in making it.

Larry wouldn't have given Bill the ship if he hadn't liked Bill very much. He was a good kid, a wonderful friend. Bill couldn't let him remain hurt.

Bill whirled, tossed the ball to Ray Colby, and ran after Larry.

"Larry!" he shouted. "Larry! Wait for me!"

6

Larry didn't wait. And he was a fast runner. His long legs carried him swiftly along the graveled driveway. Soon he was out of the park and on the sidewalk of the street. A moment later he disappeared around the corner of the block.

Bill stopped running. He stood a moment, not knowing whether to go to Larry's house, or home.

He decided to go home. Perhaps by tomorrow Larry would forget the whole thing and not be mad any more.

Bill didn't see Larry at all the next day, or the next. On Monday, though, Bill received two visitors, Tommy Wiggins and Dave Sawyer.

"We need you to pitch for us this afternoon," Tommy said seriously. "Bucky's sick. He has the measles."

Bill ran his hand through his hair. "I can't," he said.

"You can't?" echoed Dave. "Why not?"

"I've quit."

Dave stared at him. "What for?"

"I bet I know," Tommy said. "Mr. Hanley doesn't let Bill play very much. I wouldn't like that either. But, gee, Bill, you play as much as the other subs, Lee Rhodes and Kenny Shoemaker. We have to have subs, Bill. You remember what Mr. Hanley said once. It's the subs on the bench who help win games a lot of times.

"I know," said Bill. "But I can't."

Boy, if they only knew how much he really wanted to play.

33

"Come on, Bill," Tommy coaxed. "You *have* to pitch. We haven't anybody else on the team to pitch."

"And you don't want to be a quitter, do you?" Dave said.

Bill pressed his lips hard together. He didn't know what to say. No, he didn't want to be a quitter, but what should he do? He had promised Larry that he wouldn't play baseball any more. And it was wrong not to keep a promise. Everybody knew that.

But this was different, wasn't it? Who had known that Bucky would get the measles? Nobody could predict things like that.

With Bucky out of the line-up, even another pitcher would not be enough. There always had to be two pitchers on the team.

Bill thought it a long time. He had hurt Larry's feelings already. But he was sure Larry would get over it.

If he played again—if he pitched this afternoon in place of Bucky—surely Larry would understand that Bill had done that because it was his duty.

"All right," Bill said finally. "I'll pitch."

Thataboy, Bill!" cried Tommy, and slapped Bill on the shoulder. "I'm sure glad!"

Just before the game Bill warmed up with Tommy, while the other members of the team played pitch and catch among themselves, or played pepper ball. Once in a while Larry Fowler would pop into Bill's thoughts, and Bill would feel funny about playing. But at last the umpire walked out onto the field. The game started, and Bill forgot about Larry.

The Raiders batted first. Tommy, behind the plate, threw the third warmup ball to second, then walked toward Bill.

"Just throw them over, Bill," he said. "That's all you have to do."

The Raiders' leadoff man stepped to the plate. Bill eyed the target Tommy held up for him. He put his foot on the rubber, just as Ray Colby had taught him, wound up, then threw.

The batter let it go by.

"Stree-rike!" said the umpire.

Bill pitched two balls, then the batter fouled one. The next pitch was belt-high. The batter swung. Whiff!

"You're out!" cried the umpire.

7

The Raiders went scoreless the first inning. Bill felt good. If he continued like this most of the game, maybe Mr. Hanley would let him . . . Well, maybe he was just lucky that first inning.

Leadoff man Corky Davis popped out to short. Donny Swanson walked, and reached second on a wild pitch. Then Kenny Ayers drove a hot liner over the pitcher's head and Donny scored. The next two men grounded out.

The Raiders started off the second inning with two hits in succession. Bill struck out two men. But before the inning was over, three Raiders had crossed the plate.

I knew it, thought Bill. I was just lucky that first inning. But he held the Raiders down the next two innings.

In the bottom of the fourth, Sack Wilkerson punched out a single over first. Eddie Christiansen walked. Tommie Wiggins popped a fly to second for an automatic out. Then Bill came to the plate and pounded a clothesline drive through second for a single. Sack scored, and Eddie stopped on third.

Corky slammed a two-two pitch through the pitcher's box, scoring Eddie. Bill tried to reach third. The Raiders' outfielder relayed the ball in to short. The shortstop whipped the pill to third.

"Hit the dirt, Bill!" yelled the coach.

Bill slid. But the third sacker caught the ball and tagged Bill before his toe reached the sack. He was out. Donny fanned on a three-two pitch, ending the inning.

Score: Raiders – 3; Blackhawks – 3.

In the top of the fifth the Raiders had some bad luck. The first leadoff man hit a grounder to short. The ball struck the heel of Sack's glove, then bounced of his knee and rolled toward second. The runner had lots of time to reach first. But he stumbled in the baseline. He got up and raced to first. By the time his foot touched the bag, Sack had picked up the ball and thrown him out.

The next hitter doubled off Bill, a neat drive over second base. The next batter knocked a sizzling grounder down the first-base line. The ball struck the bag, and rolled toward first baseman Dave Sawyer. Dave fielded the ball and stepped on the bag for the out. The man on second went to third.

Bill worked hard on the next Raider and struck him out on a two-two pitch.

Kenny Ayers, the Blackhawks' left fielder, put on a helmet and stepped to the plate swinging two bats. He threw one aside, then clouted a chest-high pitch directly at the pitcher. One out.

Center fielder Jack Harmon walked, then ran to second on a wild pitch. Dave Sawyer also walked. Then Sack got up, and let the first two pitches go by for called strikes.

Sack stepped out of the box, rubbed his hands in the dirt, and stepped into the box again.

"Come on, Sack!" the men on the bench shouted. "A hit's a run!"

The next pitch came in. Sack stepped into it and swung.

Whiff! Sack fanned.

He turned disgustedly, tossed the bat and helmet aside.

Eddie was up next. He belted a low pitch over short, and Jack scored. Tommy flied out to left for the third out.

"Three men to go, Bill!" Dave yelled from first base. "Let's get 'em!"

The Raiders' leadoff waited till Bill

put over a strike, then laced one to third. Donny scooped the ball out of the dirt and pegged it to first for the putout. The next Raider fouled two pitches, then popped out to first. Bill worked hard on the third Raider, and struck him out with a curve ball.

The game was over. The sweat on Bill's smiling face glistened in the late afternoon sun as he walked off the field. He was tired, and happy. He looked at the stands. He hoped to see a familiar face.

Bill saw it. Ray Colby's. Ray's grin was broad, his teeth baseball-white against the golden bronze of his face. Ray waved to him.

"Nice pitching, Bill!" he said.

"Thanks," answered Bill.

Bill walked off the field. When he reached the sidewalk he stopped. His heart suddenly began to pound. The happy feeling melted away.

Looking at him from across the street was Larry Fowler. Larry spun on his heel, ran up the street and around the corner.

8

Bill was awake a lot that night thinking about Larry. He rolled and tossed in bed. He thought a lot about the game too, but always Larry would come back to his mind.

He awoke earlier than usual the next morning. His mother was surprised. She didn't have to be at work till nine o'clock. "What gets you out of bed so soon this morning?" she asked, smiling. "Didn't you sleep all night after wining that ball game?"

He didn't feel like smiling. "After breakfast I'm going over to see Larry," he said.

He didn't tell her what for.

● ● ●

Larry was on the back porch. He was putting sails on a small boat model.

"Hello, Larry," Bill greeted.

Larry turned. "Hello," he said, and kept working on the boat.

Bill watched Larry a while. He didn't quite know how to start to explain to Larry why he had played ball yesterday. He swallowed, and hitched up his pants.

"I had to play in that game yesterday, Larry," he began. "Tommy and Dave asked me to. I was the only pitcher they had."

"What was the matter with Bucky?" Larry's voice was cross.

"He's sick. He has the measles."

"Don't they have another pitcher?"

"No. Well, they *could*'ve stuck somebody else in there, I guess. But the Raiders could have knocked in twenty runs, too. I just had to pitch, Larry. I felt that I should."

Larry didn't answer.

"I might have to pitch again," Bill said. "On Thursday we're playing the Indians. But I could only pitch three innings in that game. We can't pitch more than nine innings a week."

Still Larry didn't answer.

"Please don't be mad at me, Larry," Bill went on. "I just can't quit the team like that. Not when Bucky is sick."

Larry took a deep breath. He looked at Bill. He started to say something, then clamped his lips tightly together. He picked up his boat model and walked into the house, leaving Bill standing there alone.

Bill stood looking at the door, hoping that it would open again. But it didn't. He stepped of the porch and walked through the alley to the street.

● ● ●

"Why, look who's here." The familiar voice startled Bill.

He turned and saw that it was Ray Colby. With Ray was a dark-haired woman wearing a white, polka-dotted dress.

"Hi, Ray," replied Bill. But his voice and his expression gave his feeling away.

"What's the matter, Bill?" asked Ray. "Something wrong, pal?"

Bill shook his head. "No. It's nothing."

Ray met Bill's eyes directly. He grinned, but he didn't ask Bill any more personal questions.

"This is my wife, Mary," Ray said to Bill. "This is Bill Bailey, Mary."

"Oh! I'm glad to meet you, Bill. Ray's been talking a lot about you."

"Pleased to meet you," Bill said bashfully. He couldn't understand, though, why Ray could have been talking so much about him. Guess he just likes me, thought Bill.

"We live three blocks down the street," Ray said. "How about coming down? We'll play some catch."

"Okay," said Bill.

The Colbys lived on one side of a white, double house. A lawn was in back, enclosed by a high, wire fence.

Ray Colby brought two gloves and a ball out of the house. They started to play catch.

"You remember that pitcher I was telling you about—Little Lefty?"

Bill nodded.

"I want to tell you something else about him. We had a fella by the name of Jim Woodard pitching for us in one game. He was doing all right till the ninth inning. We were two runs ahead. Suddenly the other team gets a hit, and then another. Then Jim walks a man to fill the bases. That was tough spot for anybody. Three men on, and no outs.

"Bud Herrick—that's our manager—calls time. He yanks out Jim and calls in Little Lefty to get us out of the fire. Little Lefty, mind you! A small guy, but with a lot of what it takes to make a real ball-player.

"Little Lefty walks in as if we're a-head fifteen runs. He strikes out the first man up. The next pops to short. The third batter fouls a couple of times, then fans.

Ray Colby shook his head and smiled. "You should've heard that crowd roar. I've never seen anything like it since. Never."

9

Just before eight o'clock that evening somebody rang the front doorbell. Bill answered it.

"Hello, Bill," said Larry.

Bill could hardly believe his eyes. Larry was the last person he'd expect to be ringing the doorbell. "Hello," he said.

"Can you come out a minute? I have something to ask you."

"Sure," replied Bill. He stepped out onto the small porch, closed the door softly behind him.

"I'm going to my Uncle Ben's Saturday," said Larry, his voice trembling with excitement. "Mom and Dad said you can come along if you want to.

49

Uncle Ben has a farm. He has riding horses. We can play on the farm and ride the horses all day."

Bill listened eagerly. The word "farm" built a picture of a lot of buildings in his mind. A lot of rolling hills with green grass, fences, and tall, scattered trees.

And riding a horse? He had never ridden a horse in his life. Often he had thought that he would like to. He had never dreamed, though, that someday he would be given the chance.

"Boy, that sounds good!" he said. "How long will you be gone?"

"Just for the weekend. Why don't you come along, Bill?" I'll teach you to ride. There aren't many kids who can ride horses."

Bill couldn't wait any longer. "Come in, Larry. I'll ask my mom."

Mrs. Bailey was sitting in the living room. She was knitting a sweater and watching TV.

"Mom," Bill said, "may I go with Larry to his uncle's farm tomorrow? We'll be gone just for the weekend. He has riding horses, and Larry said we can ride them all day."

Mrs. Bailey smiled. "That's nice of Larry. But are you sure it's all right with his folks, and with his uncle?"

"Oh, sure, Mrs. Bailey," Larry replied quickly. "I've already asked Mom and Dad. And I'm sure it's all right with Uncle Ben."

"Well," Mrs. Bailey said, setting aside her knitting and standing up, "I'll call up your mother anyway. It's best that us grown folks talk it over a little. Okay?"

Larry grinned. "Okay."

After a while she came back from telephoning. She smiled and said that it was all right for Bill to go.

Warmth filled Bill's heart. He hugged his mom. He didn't care if Larry watched. He loved his mom more than anything.

"Thanks, Mom," he whispered. "Thanks loads!"

Early Saturday morning the doorbell rang again. Bill ran to the door, expecting to see Larry. But it wasn't Larry. Bill's heart sank as he saw Tommy Wiggins, Dave Sawyer, and Sack Wilkerson standing on his porch. They had gloves and baseballs with them.

"Hi, Bill," said Tommy, grinning. "We're going to the field to practice. Get your glove and come along."

"Can't," replied Bill. "I'm going away,"

Tommy frowned. "Going away? Where to?"

"To Larry Fowler's uncle's farm. I'll be gone all weekend."

Behind Tommy, Dave Sawyer turned disgustedly and walked off the porch. He stopped at the bottom of the steps and glared up at Bill.

"Come on, Tommy," he said gruffly. "I told you he was a quitter."

The word stung Bill like a needle. Tommy and Sack turned away and followed Dave down the street.

A lump rose in Bill's throat. They don't understand, he thought. They just don't understand.

10

Ben Fowler's farm was twenty-three miles from Harpersville, where Bill lived. It was located high on a hill. A lake sprawled in the distance. Bill could see sailboats on it, shining like tiny mirrors as the sun touched their sails.

Ben's house was a big white building with three gables. Close to the house was a quonset-shaped barn. Beside the barn was a towering brick silo.

Bill and Larry arrived at Ben's farm at a quarter after ten. Larry's parents and his younger brother and sister came, too. They were welcomed by the loud, furious barkings of four brown dachshunds.

"Don't let them scare you," Ben Fowler said with a grin. "They're like harmless firecrackers. They just make a lot of noise."

Bill met Larry's aunt, uncle and six cousins. There were four brothers and two sisters. The two oldest brothers were much older than Larry and Bill. Ken, the third oldest brother, was about Bill's age. He was big and tanned brown as toast.

"Bill's never been on a farm before," Larry said. "Let's take him through the barn and then show him the horses."

"Sure! Let's go!"

So Bill went on his first tour of a barn. But he was disappointed. The white-washed stalls were empty. "Where are the cows?" he asked innocently.

"In pasture," replied Ken. "We only keep them in the barn during the winter. But they'll come in for milking tonight, and you can see them."

The horses were corralled on the other

side of the barn. There were four of them. One was a young, shining black colt. The colt saw the boys step on the wooden fence. He made a shrilling noise, jumped back on his thin legs, then stood still with his pointed ears perked up and his big, bright eyes wide open.

"That colt's my sister Jennie's," Ken said. "His name's Jackie."

"He beautiful," Bill said. "I wish I owned him."

Ken smiled. "And those are our riding horses—Rusty, Tony, and Pete." He looked at Bill. "Ever ride a horse?"

"Never."

"I told him I'd teach him to ride a horse if he came up here with me," Larry said.

Ken smiled. "Well, after dinner we can ride," he said. "All three are nice and gentle. Pete's mine. He's the brown one with the diamond spot on his nose. Sometimes he gets frisky and wants to run all over the place. But I've learned to handle him pretty well. Watch this. Pete! Come here, boy. Come here."

Pete's ears perked up. He turned a-round and galloped toward Ken. His long brown tail whipped and curled like a flag. He came to Ken, stopped, and stretched his head forward. Ken stroked Pete's neck, then talked to Pete as if he were talking to a person.

Bill smiled. He touched Pete with his hand. Pete looked at him. His lips curled up, showing big, white teeth, and Bill drew back.

Ken laughed. "Don't be afraid. He thinks you have something for him to eat."

Bill got over his shyness quickly. He could hardly wait for the afternoon to come so that he could ride one of the horses.

Dinnertime came and the boys were called in to eat. After dinner Ken's oldest brother, Henry, went with the boys to the corral. He saddled and bridled the horses for the boys, then left.

Ken said that Larry could ride Tony, and Bill could ride Rusty. Rusty was chestnut-colored. His tail was white and he had a large white mark on his left side.

Ken helped Bill climb into the saddle. Bill took the reins, then sat there, excitement bubbling inside him. He could hardly believe that he was sitting on a horse. And the horse seemed so big, and he seemed so high up.

"Just tug on the reins the way you want Rusty to go," said Ken. "If you want him to go right, yank on the right reins. If you want him to go left, yank on the left. Okay?"

"Okay!" Bill whispered breathlessly.

"I'll lead Rusty around a little," said Ken. "Get you used to him."

He took hold of Rusty's bridle and led

him halfway around the corral. Then he let go of the bridle, and Rusty kept walking. Bill sat with a wide smile on his lips.

Larry and Ken then climbed on their horses, and the three rode around the corral together. After a while Ken o-pened the gate and the boys rode their horses out to the rolling, green meadow. For the next two hours they just rode and rode. At first the boys, led by Ken, had their horses walk. Later they put their animals into a jog trot.

"How do you like it?" Larry asked Bill.

"Great!" exclaimed Bill.

After church the next morning the three boys went horseback riding again. They rode far out into the meadow. They ap-proached a fence made of crisscrossed logs. The fence separated the field they

59

were on from another field through which a creek flowed.

"Let's water the horses," Larry suggested.

"Okay," replied Ken.

It was like the real West, thought Bill, where cowboys rode their horses for long hours then stopped to water them.

Ken turned his animal around. Larry and Bill followed him. Ken's horse leaped over the fence first. Then Larry's. Finally Bill's.

But as Bill's horse went over Bill lost his balance and fell. As he hit the ground he screamed.

11

Bill rose to his feet, his blue jeans soiled. His left arm hurt. He tried to move it. It hurt worse.

Ken and Larry reined their horses quickly toward him. They climbed out of their saddles. Larry's face was white. "Are you hurt, Bill?" he cried.

"My arm's hurt," murmured Bill.

"We must get him home, Ken," said Larry. "He might have to go to a doctor."

"I'll get on the other side of the fence," said Ken.

He had Pete leap back over the fence, then helped Bill climb up on Pete. Bill put his right arm around Ken's waist.

"I hope it isn't bad, Bill," said Larry,

worriedly. "It's all my fault if it is."

"Don't worry," said Bill. "It doesn't hurt *too* much."

Ken had Pete trot back across the meadow toward home. On the way a horrifying thought took hold of Bill. It was his pitching arm that had been hurt!

Ken told his father what had happened. Immediately Ben Fowler had Bill get into his station wagon and drove him five miles to a doctor. Larry, his father, and Ken went along.

The doctor, a small, white-haired man with glasses, asked Bill to remove his shirt. He looked the arm over carefully. He pressed his thumb and forefinger around the elbow, and Bill winced.

"Oh-oh," said the doctor. "I think I know what it is, but I'll x-ray your arm to make sure."

Bill stared. "Did—did it break, doctor?"

"Could have," said the doctor. "Come in here."

He led Bill into a white-walled room in which was a large, black machine. Larry, Ken, and both of their fathers followed Bill in.

"Rest your arm on this table, Bill," said the doctor.

Bill tried, but it hurt so much the doctor had to help him. The doctor worked around the machine awhile, then said, "All right, Bill. Sit in the other room. We have to wait for the picture to develop."

About twenty minutes later the doctor came out, carrying a large, square film. He held it up so that everybody could see it. All Bill could see were some wide, ghostlike lines and a ball-like spot.

"This film will show you what's happened to Bill's elbow," said the doctor. "The elbow is chipped. He was very fortunate." He smiled at Bill. "You may not like this, Bill, but it'll be necessary if you want the arm to heal as quickly as possible. I'll have to put a cast on it."

Bill's eyes widened. His hopes sank. "Can't I pitch any more?"

"Pitch baseball?" The doctor grinned. "Not for a while, Bill. Not for about a month, anyway. But be back here in three weeks. I'll take the cast off then."

12

The doctor put Bill's arm into a white plaster cast. Then he put the arm in a sling. The cast came only to Bill's wrist so that he could move his thumb and fingers.

Larry and his parents took Bill home Sunday afternoon. They felt real bad about Bill's hurt arm. Especially Larry. He kept close to Bill and just looked at him without saying anything. His eyes were red, unhappy.

Bill's mother stared at the plaster cast on Bill's arm.

"Bill had an accident," Mrs. Fowler explained. "It's not too serious. A bone in his elbow was chipped when he fell off a horse."

"It doesn't hurt at all, Mom," said Bill. "And the doctor said it'll be all healed up in three weeks."

"The three boys were out in the fields, riding horses," Mrs. Fowler said quietly to Bill's mother. "My brother's boy Ken, Larry, and Bill. I guess they had wanted their horses to get a drink of water. In order to get to the water the horses had to jump over a fence. Bill fell off when his horse jumped."

"We're very sorry about it, Dorothy," Mrs. Fowler said. "The boys shouldn't have had their horses jump over fences."

Mrs. Bailey smiled. "Well, it was an accident, and it wasn't too serious," she said good-naturedly. "Thank God for that. But I know how Bill always wanted to ride a horse." She turned to Bill. "Think you'll ever want to ride again?"

Bill's eyes widened. "Why sure, Mom! It's fun. This chipped elbow isn't going to stop me. The next time I'll make sure I hang on tighter!"

Everybody roared out in laughter.

The Fowlers left in better spirits than when they had brought Bill. Bill was glad. But he had known all the time that his mother wouldn't get mad. She just wasn't the get-mad kind. Not when it came to accidents like falling off a horse.

Corky Davis, Donny Swanson, and Tommy Wiggins came over the next day to visit him. They said they'd heard that he had fallen off a horse.

Then Tommy said, "We had a practice game with the Cardinals yesterday. They're in another league."

"How'd you make out?" asked Bill.

"We lost by two runs."

"Think you'll be able to pitch any more?" Corky asked.

"Oh, sure," said Bill with confidence.

"The doctor said the cast could come off in three weeks. With some practice I could play again."

"Boy, that's swell!"

"Yes, but by then we'll probably be at the bottom of the league," Tommy said unhappily. "Good thing Bucky's almost over his measles. He can pitch for us next week."

Later in the afternoon the other members of the Blackhawks' team came to see Bill. They brought him a card, signed by every player. Also a big, square, heavy package.

Bill anxiously opened the package. It was a box of chocolate candy. Bill passed the box around to the boys. Each took a candy. Each enjoyed it, too.

Bill was anxious to see the Blackhawks play the Eagles Tuesday. But the game was rained out. It would be played on

Friday, the day for postponed games. He didn't have anything to do, so he read five chapters of a baseball book. After the rain he walked outside. The air felt fresh and cool. He was glad. The weather had sure been hot.

Bill hoped he wouldn't meet Ray Colby. What would Ray think if he saw that cast on Bill's arm and learned what had happened? He might get disgusted and not bother with Bill any more.

Ray must have liked Bill very much, or he wouldn't have taught Bill how to stand in the pitcher's box, or tell him a lot about that pitcher, Little Lefty. Guess Little Lefty must have been a wonderful pitcher for someone to remember him like that and talk so much about him.

On Wednesday Larry came over. Bill hadn't seen him since Sunday.

"Where have you been, Larry?" Bill

asked. "I haven't seen you."

"Home, most of the time," answered Larry. "Working on my boat model. You —you're not mad at me, are you, Bill?"

Bill frowned. "Mad? Why should I be mad at you?"

Larry looked long at Bill, then blinked his eyes and looked away.

"Because it was my fault that you have your arm in a cast," he said. "And I know how crazy you are about baseball. And now you can't play."

13

Bill met Roy Colby at the Blackhawks-Eagles game on Friday. Ray stared at the cast on Bill's arm.

"What are you carrying there?" he asked with a puzzled look.

"I chipped my elbow," replied Bill. "Fell of a horse." Bill went on to explain what had happened.

"You sure met up with some tough luck," said Ray. "But it could've been worse. Think you'll be able to play baseball any more this year?"

"Oh, sure. The doctor said after three weeks he'll take the cast off."

"But you wont be able to play right after the cast is off," said Ray. "You'll have to exercise that arm gradually." Ray put a hand inside the sling and rested it on the cast. "After the doc takes that cast off, don't you do anything with that arm yourself. Let me help you with it. Okay?"

Bill grinned. "Okay, Ray."

They sat together watching the game, and gave the Blackhawks a lot of voice support. Bucky Myers was pitching. He started off with a bad inning. He walked the first two men up, then gave two straight hits. A man flied out, but the next man doubled. Four runs crossed the plate before the Blackhawks buckled down and got the Eagles out.

The Blackhawks didn't score till the third inning, when Jack Harmon tripled to left and Dave Sawyer knocked him in with a single. Bucky laced into a low pitch for a double over second. Dave made the turn at third as the ball was relayed from the outfield to the shortstop.

He slid safely into home for the second run.

Sack Wilkerson hit a high foul ball which the catcher caught. Eddie grounded out to short. Then Tommy arched one out to deep right center.

Ray Colby rose to his feet. "That ball is labeled!" he yelled.

Bill rose beside him. "Thatago, Tommy!" he yelled.

Bucky scored. The Eagles' center fielder finally picked up the ball, relayed it to the second baseman. The second baseman hurled it home.

It was too late for the play. Tommy Wiggins crossed the plate for a home run to tie the score.

The Blackhawks and the Eagles held each other from getting more runs as they went into the sixth inning. The Eagles, first up, went down – one, two, three. Then the Blackhawks – one, two, three.

The game was forced into an extra inning. Again the Eagles came to bat. Bucky walked the first man. He fanned the next. Then Corky nabbed a hot clothesline drive for the second out, and picked off the runner at first for a quick double-play.

Dave Sawyer, first man up in the seventh for the Blackhawks, doubled with a hot grounder over the third-base sack. Bucky flied out and Sack fanned. The Eddie laced a line drive over the short-stop's head. Dave made the turn at third and came in, standing up, to win the ball game.

Bill and Ray walked away from the game, smiling happily.

"That was a good game," said Ray. "Reminds me of the time when we played the Huxton Falcons. Little Lefty was pitching that game, too. We went into the ninth to tie the score. Then the tenth, the eleventh, the twelfth. Little

Lefty stuck right in there like a giant."

Ray went on, spinning another interesting tale about Little Lefty before they reached the corner where he went his way, and Bill went his.

After supper Bill relaxed in the living room. He began thinking about the ball game. He looked at his hand sticking out of the cast. He wiggled his thumb and fingers. He struck the cast gently with his other hand, and sadly shook his head.

Only five days had passed so far since he had hurt his elbow. Five days—not even a week—and it seemed like a month. He had two weeks and two days to go yet.

He closed his mouth tightly and tried not to think about it. But he couldn't help thinking about baseball.

Suddenly he remembered the promise he had made Larry. Whatever had made him think he would continue playing baseball once his arm was all right?

Bill swallowed. What a promise to make! What a terrible, terrible promise!

The doorbell rang.

"I'll get it, Mom!" Bill said.

He went to the door, opened it. It was Larry. He was carrying a large, flat package.

"Hi, Bill," he said, and smiled. He lifted the package. "Here. My dad bought this for you."

"For me?" He took the package and opened it with quick, nervous fingers.

Inside the package was a brand-new baseball glove.

"My dad bought me one, too," Larry said brightly. "Just like yours, but for a right-hander."

14

Never had days gone by so slowly. When the last two days of the third week came around, Bill began to count the hours.

At last Saturday arrived. Mr. Fowler drove Bill to the doctor. Larry and Mrs. Bailey went along.

The doctor removed the cast from Bill's arm. He looked at the elbow carefully, moved Bill's arm back and forth. Bill didn't feel a thing, just a little numbness.

The doctor grinned. "Well, Bill, looks like the elbow is as good as new again. But don't get too anxious with it. Exercise it gradually and easily. In a week or so you can be back on the mound, pitching."

Bill sighed with relief. It sure felt good not to have that heavy plaster on his arm any more.

Bill's mother would not let him play catch till Sunday afternoon. She allowed him to play then only because he teased so much.

"My elbow's okay, Mom!" he said. "It feels fine!"

Mrs. Bailey shook her head. "I guess you'll grow up to be just like your father," she said. "He sure loved the game, too."

Bill looked curiously at his mother. He'd been a very little boy when his father died. He remembered a few things about his father that his mother had told him. He had been a bus driver, a gas station owner, and finally an automobile mechanic. He had liked all kinds of sports, too. Hunting, fishing, golfing, and yes—baseball. Bill couldn't remember what position his father had played, though. Guess his mother had never told him that.

"What position did Dad play, Mom?" Could *you* remember?"

She smiled for a moment, and her blue eyes twinkled. "Oh, yes. He was a pitcher."

Bill's eyes widened. "He was?" He stared breathlessly at his mother. "Was he good, Mom? Was he real good?"

His mother laughed. "You bet he was. Why, I think he was considered the best pitcher in the league one year."

"Gosh, Mom!" exclaimed Bill. "You never told me that."

"I think I have," she said. "But you were too small to remember. Everybody used to call your father 'Lefty'—'Little Lefty.' Because he wasn't very big."

15

Manager Hanley had Bill start on the mound in the game against the Raiders. Bill's arm was feeling good now, He had played pitch and catch with Larry and Ray Colby. He had thrown several times in batting practice. The arm felt good as new.

Bill walked a man in the first inning, and gave up one run to the Raiders. The Blackhawks got a man on in the bottom of the first. He reached third on an error made by the Raiders' shortstop, but nobody knocked him in.

Bill went out to the mound feeling more sure of himself than he had when the game started. He remembered to wind up and deliver as Ray had coached him to do. His control was fairly good. A man grounded out. Another reached first safely on an error by third baseman Donny Swanson. Then a long fly was hit to left. The runner on first raced to second. Kenny Ayers sprinted hard after the ball. He stretched out his glove and speared it. Then he turned and pegged the ball to second.

Shortstop Sack Wilkerson caught the throw-in, whipped it to first. The runner was out before he could tag up.

Three outs.

"Nice play, Kenny!" the boys shouted as Kenny ran in from the outfield. A happy grin was on his face. Bill shook his hand.

"Thanks, Kenny," he said. "You pulled me out of that hole!"

Dave Sawyer led off the bottom half of the second with a line drive over second base. Sack struck out. Then Dale

Seligman, who was playing right field in place of Eddie Christiansen, hit a fly to center field. The Raiders' outfielder backed up a dozen steps, reached out his glove, and made a one-hand catch. Then Tommy Wiggins came up.

Tommy belted a low pitch to the second baseman. The ball zipped through the player's legs and rolled to the outfield. Dave rounded second and raced for third. The play was made on him and Tommy scrambled to second. Both were safe.

Then Bill walloped a high pitch over the first baseman's head and both runners scored. Corky Davis fanned to end the inning.

Score: Blackhawks – 2, Raiders – 1.

Bill returned to the mound with a smile on his lips. He was pitching a good game. And he had knocked in two runs. If he and his teammates would keep hitting that apple as they had in that second inning, the Blackhawks would walk away with the game in their pocket.

The first Raider let the first pitch go for a called strike. The next throw was over the outside corner. The Raider put out his bat and laid down a perfect bunt just inside the third-base line.

The second Raider bunted, too! Donny was playing in close, but not close enough to pick up the ball and throw out the hitter.

"Come on, Bill, boy!" Tommy shouted. "Let's get 'em!"

Manager Hanley yelled to Dave Sawyer to play in close, too, in case of another bunt. The next batter didn't bunt, though. He stepped into Bill's pitch and whacked it for a double to left center. Both runners scored.

Bill stood nervously on the mound. No matter what kind of pitch he threw, a Raider got on base. He threw four pitches to the batter. None were over the plate.

"Take your base!" said the umpire.

Men on first and second . . . Bill's heart pounded. He stretched, delivered. Another bunt! Donny ran in, picked up the ball, heaved it first. The throw was wild. The runner on second scored.

"Settle down!" yelled Manager Hanley, "Make those throws good!"

Crack! A long, high fly to the outfield. Kenny chased after it. Jack Harmon chased after it. The ball cleared the fence for a home run.

"Time!" yelled Manager Hanley. "Bill! Come out. Bucky, take over!"

Bill walked off the mound, his head bowed. Tears burned in his eyes. It was the worst game he had ever pitched. The worst.

16

The Raiders defeated the Blackhawks 11 to 4. After the game Bill was starting to walk home when he heard his name called.

"Hey, Bill! Wait a minute!"

It was Ray Colby. With Ray was Larry. Larry was carrying his new glove.

"How about staying for a while and practicing on your control?" asked Ray. "Also seems as if you, Dave, and Donny could use some practice fielding bunts. How about it?"

Bill shrugged. "I don't know. Maybe Mr. Hanley won't let me pitch any more, anyway."

"I heard that," a voice said behind

him. "And you're one hundred percent wrong."

Bill swung around. His face got red.

"I think Ray's suggestion is excellent," said Manager Hanley. His gray eyes were sparkling with cheerfulness, even though his team had lost. "You were doing all right those first couple of innings, Bill. Then they started to bunt and you became flustered. Some practice on fielding those bunts will help us out. A pitcher has as much to do in fielding bunts as the third and first baseman, you know."

"Okay," replied Bill. "I'll stay."

Manager Hanley called to Dave and Donny. "Get in your positions," he told the boys. "Ray, you get in the batter's box. You were a lot better at that than I was," he added, grinning.

Ray, laughed. "I've put on a few years!" he said. But he stepped into the batter's box. Bill, on the mound, wound up and delivered. Ray laid the bunt on the grass toward third bas. Donny fielded the ball, pegged it to first.

"Bill," said Ray, "you hardly moved off the pitcher's box. Run after that ball, too. You could've fielded it before Donny did. Quite often a split second makes a difference between a hit and an out."

Bill nodded. On the next play he fielded the bunt, threw to first.

"That's it," said Frank Hanley. "Nice play, Bill."

They worked out for half an hour. Bill was tired and perspired freely, but he had enjoyed every minute of it.

"Okay, boys," said Manager Hanley. "That'll be enough. Go home and have your supper."

"Larry, will you come over afterwards?" Bill asked as they walked home together. I want to practice on my control."

Larry's face brightened. "I sure will!" he said.

After supper Larry came over to Bill's house. He missed a lot of Bill's pitches. But he seemed to love playing pitch and catch. Bill could hardly believe it. Larry had never liked baseball at all. Now he seemed like a different boy. He acted as though he had discovered something pretty wonderful.

17

The baseball season moved into the middle of August. The Raiders led the league. The Blackhawks were in second place, followed by the Indians, with the Eagles trailing in last place.

Bill pitched the first three innings of the game against the Indians. He allowed three hits and three runs. Bucky finished the game. The Blackhawks took it 7 to 5.

Bill remained after the game. Larry came from the stands with Ray Colby.

"Pitched a nice game, Bill," said Ray.

Bill smiled. "Thanks," he said.

"You're getting to look more and more like Little Lefty," said Ray, lighting his pipe. "You're gaining confidence in yourself. All you need to do is work on your control."

Bill looked up at Ray. "Did Little Lefty ever have trouble with *his* control?"

"Oh, sure he did," said Ray. "We had to take him out once because he was so wild. Just couldn't get the ball anywhere near the plate."

"What did you do?"

"I worked on him," answered Ray seriously. "I had him throw to me till he was blue in the face. You should have seen the size of my hand when we'd finished! But it did him good. He got so he could throw that pill at any spot over the plate he wanted to."

"I know," Bill said.

Ray looked at him curiously. Then a grin crossed his lips. "You knew?" he said. "You mean you knew all the time who it was I've been talking about?"

"I didn't know until a few days ago,"

replied Bill. "Mom told me."

"I would've told you, myself, pretty soon," said Ray quietly.

Dave Sawyer, Donny Swanson, Tommy Wiggins, and some of the substitute players remained after the ball game. Frank Hanley could not stay. But Bill didn't mind; Ray Colby was staying.

They practiced fielding bunts. Then they practiced batting. Larry batted, too. Ray coached him about where to stand in the box. Larry did not seem to have much trouble. He wasn't afraid of a pitched ball, either. He stepped into it and took his cut. Sometimes he'd hit the ball; sometimes he wouldn't.

Then Ray Colby knocked out fly balls. Larry chased them in the outfield, too. Some of the flies he misjudged. Some struck his glove and bounced out. Some he caught.

Bill watched with interest. Larry was taking to baseball like a duck to water. And the way Larry chased after the ball and threw it showed that someday he would make a good ballplayer.

The boys were pretty exhausted when Ray Colby finally said, "Okay, boys. Let's call it quits."

Larry and Bill walked home together. Both of them were sweating from running so much. But Larry seemed more tired. Bill knew Larry had run around much more than he had.

"Bill," said Larry, breathlessly, "do you think that—" He paused. "Oh, never mind."

Bill stared at him. "Think what?" he said.

"It's crazy," replied Larry. "I wouldn't have a chance."

Bill frowned. "Have a chance at what?"

Larry looked at him. His eyes were

wide and serious. "A chance to play on the team. Do you think I would, Bill?"

Their eyes locked. "I don't know, Larry," said Bill, thoughtfully. "But you might. You really might."

18

Bill still had not pitched a full six-inning game since he had chipped his elbow. Manager Frank Hanley had him pitch either the first three innings of a game, or the last three. Or Bucky Myers would pitch the whole game himself.

I wonder if Dad had the same trouble when he was a kid that I'm having, Bill thought. I wonder how old he was when he began to pitch a full game. But maybe he was a lot better than I am. Maybe he was a *natural*.

Bill sat on the bench as the Blackhawks-Raiders game went into the last inning, the Blackhawks leading. He remembered that moment yesterday when

Larry had asked him if he thought he, Larry, might have a chance to play on the team. Larry, of all guys. Larry, who Bill had once thought cared for nothing except ship-in-a-bottle models.

After the game, which the Blackhawks lost 7 to 6, Bill approached Manager Hanley.

"Mr. Hanley," he said, "Larry Fowler would like to play on our team. Can he, or is it too late?"

Frank Hanley stroked his ear thoughtfully. "I don't know. I think it is too late, but I can ask the program director, Charlie Weston. Who is Larry Fowler?"

"A good friend of mine," replied Bill. "He had never liked baseball. But a little while ago his father bought him a glove and he's been practicing with us. He's that boy with glasses."

The manager smiled. "Oh, I know. Larry. Of course. He needs a lot of practice, but he's got the makings of a ballplayer."

Bill's eyes brightened. "He'd be happy to get in just an inning or so," he said.

"I imagine he would," Frank Hanley said. He patted Bill on the shoulder. "I'll see Charlie tomorrow. If he says Larry can play with us, I'll let you know. How's that?"

Bill grinned. "That's fine!"

Bill told Larry about his talk with Manager Hanley.

"Boy!" muttered Larry hopefully. "I sure hope I can play!"

Bill smiled. "You like baseball pretty well now, don't you?"

"Yes, I do. I guess I never thought it was so much fun."

Bill and Larry could hardly wait till the next evening. Both went to watch the Eagles play the Raiders, expecting to see either Manager Hanley there, or the program director, Charlie Weston.

The boys were disappointed. Neither man was present.

But when Bill returned home his mother had news for him. "Bill," she said, "Frank Hanley called. He said to tell you to bring Larry Fowler to the next game."

"You mean Larry could play with us?"

His mother shrugged. "That's the way I understand the message," she said, and smiled broadly.

"Oh, boy!" Bill shouted. "Wait till Larry hears that!"

In the fifth inning of the game against the Eagles, Frank Hanley put in Larry in place of right fielder Eddie Christiansen. The Blackhawks were leading the Eagles by one run. On the mound for the Blackhawks was Bucky Myers. So far he had pitched the whole game.

Bucky fanned the first man up. The

second batter belted a high fly to right center. Both Jack Harmon and Larry chased after it. Larry arrived under it first. He yelled for it, just as he was coached to do.

The ball came down, struck his glove, and bounced to the ground. A groan rose from the stands. The runner raced to second.

Bill shifted nervously on the bench. That high fly would have been a nice one for Larry to have caught. But it was high—real high. Jack might even have missed it, himself.

The Eagles' next man hit a high-bounding grounder through the pitcher's box. The ball bounded to the outfield, scoring the man on second. The hitter held up on first.

The score was tied up, 5 and 5.

Bill looked at Frank Hanley. The manager had his mouth closed tight. He shook his head a couple of times, picked up a handful of dirt and threw it down again.

He's probably thinking about Larry, thought Bill. He's probably wishing he hadn't put Larry in there.

19

Bucky Myers toed the rubber, looked at the runner on first base, then threw to the plate. The pitch was wild. The ball sailed past catcher Tommy Wiggins' mitt and bounded against the backstop screen. The Eagles' runner advanced to second.

The Blackhawks' infielders began to chatter loud and hard.

"Take your time, Bucky!"

"Put 'em over, boy!"

Bucky pitched again. "Ball two!"

Then Bucky threw in a slow pitch. A change-up. The batter waited for it, then swung. Whack! The ball zoomed like a rocket to right field. It was a hit. Larry ran in a few steps, caught the ball on the first hop, then pegged it to Bucky. Bucky caught it, spun on his heels and whipped the ball home. The runner slid, just as Tommy put the ball on him.

Up went the umpire's thumb. "You're out!" he shouted.

Everybody on the Blackhawks' bench rose to his feet. They shouted, clapped their hands, and slapped each others' shoulders.

"Thataway to go, Tommy!"

"Nice play, Bucky!"

"That was a nice peg Larry made, too," Frank Hanley said, smiling. "Don't forget that!"

Bill looked at him. That certainly had been a nice peg. Eddie Christiansen, who was the regular right fielder, was smiling, too. He wasn't jealous at all that Larry had taken his place, or that Larry had made that fine throw.

Two outs. Runner on second base.

Buck worked on the batter. None of

the first three pitches went over the plate. The fourth pitch was a strike. Then the batter swung at a low pitch. *Crack!* The ball ripped across the grass between third and short and rolled to Kenny Ayers in left field. The runner on second raced to third, started for home.

Kenny reached for the ball. Just then the ball took a bad hop; it must have hit a stone. It bounded over Kenny's arm and rolled against the fence.

Kenny tore after it. He pegged it home. But a run had scored, and the second runner was standing on second.

The next batter popped out to Sack Wilkerson to end the Eagles' hitting streak.

But the damage was done. The Eagles were ahead 6 to 5.

Manager Hanley turned to Bill. "Bill, take a ball and get out in the bull pen with Eddie. Loosen up."

Bill's eyes widened. "Yes, sir!" he

said. He picked a ball out of the bag and went behind the dugout with Eddie. He started his throws easily, then gradually harder. Every once in a while he stopped a moment to see what was happening in the game.

Donny Swanson, first man up for the Blackhawks, started the ball rolling. He singled through short. Then Kenny laid down a bunt, fooling the Eagles' infielders, who were playing deep.

Two men on. Jack Harmon up. He popped to the infield for an automatic out.

Bill shook his head. He gave up hope of playing in this game. It was too close, a pitcher's duel. Manager Hanley wouldn't put him in there now.

Dave Sawyer stepped to the plate and belted a shoulder-high pitch over the right fielder's head. The Blackhawks' fans leaped up in the bleachers and screamed their throats dry as Donny and

Kenny crossed the plate. Dave tried to stretch the long hit into a homer. But the ball was in the infield by now, and the coach called him back to third.

Score: Eagles – 6; Blackhawks – 7.

Then the Eagles' pitcher bore down. He struck out Bucky. And Sack hit a dribbling grounder to third for an easy out.

The Eagles came to bat full of pep and eagerness. They waited till Bucky pitched a strike before they would swing. And Bucky's pitches weren't good. The plate seemed too small for his throws.

He walked the first two men, and then the next man bunted to fill the bases.

Bucky was sweating as he stood behind the rubber. The Eagles' fans were yelling.

"A hit! That's all we need—just a hit!"

Bucky took off his cap and mopped his face with it. He put it back on, then dropped the ball. He sure was nervous.

"Time!" yelled Manager Hanley. He rose, looked behind the dugout, and settled his gaze on Bill Bailey.

"Okay, Bill. Get in there and get 'em out, boy!"

20

Bill could hardly believe his ears. Top of the sixth inning. The bases loaded. No outs. And he was asked to pitch?

It didn't seem possible. Yet, what good was Bucky? He was wild as a lion. He'd probably walk the whole ball park if he were kept in there.

A clamor of voices rose as Bucky came out and Bill went in.

"Who's the little fella?" one of the Eagles' fans shouted. "He doesn't look big enough to be a mascot!"

Bill tried not to listen to them.

"Don't be a rabbit-ears," Ray Colby had told him. "Never pay attention to what people yell at you. They just want to get you jittery so you can't throw."

Bill threw in some warmup pitches to Tommy. Tommy smiled at him.

"Thataboy, Bill!" he said. "Let's go after 'em!"

Bill stepped to the mound, got the signal from Tommy, and made the stretch. Swish! The ball sped over the heart of the plate.

"Strike!" snapped the umpire.

The next pitch was slightly inside. The right-hand hitter swung, fouled to the backstop screen.

The next two pitches were balls. The next was a curve. The batter cut at it. Whiff!

One out!

"Two more to go, Bill, ol' kid!" muttered Tommy behind his mask. "Just two more!"

The second batter slid his hand along the handle of the bat as if to bunt—then stepped back quickly.

"Strike one!" said the umpire.

Bill's pitches were good. The ball was going almost exactly where he wanted it to. Those hours he had practiced on his control were paying off.

Another pitch was streaking for the center of the plate. The batter swung. Crack! A solid wallop! The white pill rocketed across the infield less than five feet high. Sack Wilkerson waited for it, caught it. He looked at second, third— but the men had tagged up.

Two outs. The infield chatter grew louder and louder. The sound in the stands had almost died away to nothing.

"One more," murmured Tommy. "Just one more, Bill!"

Bill took a deep breath. *A small guy, but with a lot of what it takes to make a real ballplayer*, Ray Colby had once said about Bill's father. I want to be like him, Bill thought.

He toed the rubber, stretched, threw.

Ball one!

Tommy carried the ball partway to Bill, then threw it the rest of the distance. The next pitch was another ball.

"Come on, Bill! Throw 'em over!"

That voice came from the bleachers. Bill would recognize it anywhere. It was Ray Colby's. Ray, who had taught him more about pitching than anybody else. Ray, who used to catch for Bill's dad, Little Lefty.

"Stee—rike!"

Another pitch, curving in fast. The batter only looked at it.

"Strike two!"

Two and two.

Bill's heart pounded. He was scared. He had to get another strike past that batter. He had to.

Bill toed the rubber, stretched. The batter swung at the pitch. Crack!

A solid drive over third! Bill's heart sank. The runners tore around the bases.

One run scored! Two! The Eagles went ahead!

Then suddenly a voice boomed over the cheers coming from the Eagles' fans.

"Foul ball!"

Bill stared. A shiver went down his back. What a lifesaver! He took another deep breath, and sighed with relief.

He looked at the batter. The count was still two and two. Bill stepped to the rubber, looked at the plate, at Tommy's mitt, and threw.

The ball sailed like a small white rocket toward the outside of the plate. It curved in sharply, just as the batter swung.

Smack! The ball landed in Tommy's mitt.

"Strike three!" yelled the umpire.

Three outs!

The Blackhawks' fans screamed.

Tommy rushed out to the mound and wrapped his arms around Bill. "You did it, Bill!" he shouted. "You did it!"

Then the whole team ganged around Bill and hugged him.

"You're the best pitcher in the league, Bill!" Larry said fondly. "I'm sure glad I'm playing with you!"

Bill smiled. He was trembling all over. He had never felt so happy in his life. "So am I," he said.

Manager Hanley shook his hand. And then Ray Colby was there, his face spread in a wide, happy grin.

"Nice pitching, Little Lefty!" he said proudly.

Bill felt a lump come to his throat. But he swallowed it and said bravely, "Thanks, Ray!"

CPSIA information can be obtained at www.ICGtesting.com
Printed in the USA
BVOW08s2041031213

337887BV00004B/12/P